What do the grown-ups do?

Gordon the Wildlife Filmmaker

"To say that I was totally enamoured by the 'What do' series is something of an understatement. I always feel that the ultimate test lies in how one's own children treat such reading materials. When I asked them if they were enjoying the books, they were unequivocal in their praise of them. In these days of increasing complexity and technological pressures, it is a sheer delight to have something as precious as these books to relate to with the children."
Pocketful of Rye.

"Really detailed and informative books, which contain exactly the questions that intelligent children ask and adults are often unable to answer. There is fun, humour and a wonderful sense of place too."
Dr Ken Greig, Rector, Hutchesons' Grammar School.

"What makes these books noteworthy are the practical details from the mouths of the real workers, which fascinate rather than bore. It's eye-opening stuff."
Teach Primary magazine.

"As a series of books, they are incredibly impressive and from a debut author simply brilliant."
Chopsy Baby.

"Older readers will find these true-to-life tales absolutely fascinating. And that's the beauty of these books. They target children aged 5-10 but they can be explored on several levels."
Madhouse Family Reviews.

What do the grown-ups do?

Gordon the
Wildlife Filmmaker

Mairi McLellan

Matador
9 Priory Business Park
Kibworth Beauchamp
Leicestershire LE8 0RX, UK
Tel: (+44) 116 279 2299
Fax: (+44) 116 279 2277
Email: books@troubador.co.uk
Web: www.troubador.co.uk/matador

ISBN: 978 1784621 865

Editor: Eleanor MacCannell

British Library Cataloguing in Publication Data.
A catalogue record for this book is available from the British Library.

Printed and bound by Gutenberg Press, Malta

Matador is an imprint of Troubador Publishing Ltd

www.kidseducationalbooks.com

What do the grown-ups do?

Dear Reader,

What do the grown-ups do? is a series of books designed to educate children about the workplace using chatty, light-hearted stories, written through the eyes of the children.

The aim is to encourage a positive work ethic from a young age, to broaden their minds to the world around them, and to help motivate them to learn more about the jobs that interest them. I hope that by introducing these concepts early, it will make a small contribution to preparing them for their life ahead. It's just a start, and at this age, although the message is serious, it is designed to be fun.

For younger children who will be doing a combination of reading and being read to, this series will be reasonably challenging. I have deliberately tried not to over-simplify them too much in order to maintain reality, whilst keeping the tone chatty and informal.

The books can be read in any order but they are probably best starting from the beginning. The order of the series can be found at the back of this book. Many more will be coming soon so please check the website for updates: **www.kidseducationalbooks.com**.

I hope you enjoy them.

Happy reading!

Mairi

A note of thanks to Gordon - my first flatmate and a truly charismatic, energetic, honest and witty individual. He's tread where most are too scared to roam and brought wonderful, innovative footage from the wilderness to our living room. The Isle of Mull should be very proud of its exports.

A note of thanks also to the kind folk who contributed to the photos of Gordon's adventures:

Paul Williams
Jonny Young
Johnny Rogers
Rowan Musgrave
Saritha Wilkinson
Susanna Handslip
Giles Badger
Theo Webb
Graham MacFarlane
Justine Evans
Jonny Keeling
Gordon Buchanan

This has saved me a great deal of travelling, not to mention close encounters with animals that I am not equipped for! I greatly appreciate it.

Life by the sea in Badaneel

Badaneel, in the Northwest Highlands of Scotland, was home to the Mackenzie girls, Ava, Skye and Gracie. The twins, Ava and Skye, were seven years old and their sister, Gracie, was just a year younger. They lived in one of the most beautiful parts of Scotland and roamed wild as the heather amongst the mountains, beaches and glens of Badaneel.

Playing by the sea in Badaneel.

The children were always playing outside and especially loved the sea. They could spend hours on the beach – playing rounders, jumping in the waves, or building dams by the river. Today was particularly exciting as they were going off to sea for a week! Their parents had hired a boat and had promised that they would see all sorts of wildlife on their trip, including strange sheep, dolphins, seals, puffins, gannets and maybe even a minke whale!

Their first trip took them to St Kilda and, as was typical in the Scottish summer, the weather was very changeable. The mist had come down, as thick as pea soup, and it felt as if they had sailed for days before they finally reached the remote islands.

"There they are!" shouted Mother.

Ava saw them too, appearing out of the mist like something from another world. St Kilda was no longer inhabited, except by one of the world's largest gannet populations.

"I've never seen so many birds!" exclaimed Ava.

The cliffs appear through the mist at St Kilda.

Gannets! White birds with dark tips on their wings, known for high-speed diving!

The birds were nesting in the rocks.

"In the olden days, the men from St Kilda used to climb the rocks, using ropes made from cow hides," said Mother. "They captured sea-birds, especially young gannets, known as *gugas*, and fulmars. The women of St Kilda took puffins from their burrows, and ate them as a snack, just like you might eat an apple! The St Kildans were known as the *bird people* because that was their main diet," smiled Mother.

The girls were mesmerised by St Kilda. So many birds, lots of old ruins, massive cliffs and giant caves. They could have spent weeks exploring, but time was short and they only had the afternoon.

Ashore they saw the *cleits*, which were stone structures used to air-dry and store the birds as winter food. The people who lived here had to work in the same way as animals, by storing food from the summer to use in the winter. *It must have been a hard life on this remote rock of an island,* thought Skye, but there was a sense of peace and calm, and the views were fabulous.

Stone cleits - rather like an olden-day cellar.

"As well as being used for meat, the rest of the bird was also used to make various things," explained Father. "They used the feathers to fill pillows and bedding; the skin from the gannets to make shoes; the oil from the birds' stomachs for cooking and lamp oil, and even as medicine."

Skye was watching in amazement. "Mama," she said. "You know how we have been investigating grown-ups jobs?"

"Yes," replied Mother.

"Well, I was wondering. Is there a job where you get to look for wild birds and animals?"

Village Bay in the mist – ruins of homes and cleits.

"Funny you should ask, Skye," replied Mother. "I think you are going to find this holiday very interesting. After St Kilda we are visiting a place called Tobermory on the Isle of Mull."

"You mean the place where Balamory is filmed?" asked Skye excitedly.

"Yes," laughed Mother," but this is the real Tobermory and it's just as pretty as the pictures. Tobermory is where my friend Gordon Buchanan lives. Gordon is now a well-known wildlife filmmaker. He travels the world, filming different animals, many of them hard to find and often quite scary!" said Mother.

"Oh wow!" said Skye. Ava and Gracie had been listening in.

"Can we meet him, Mama? Please!" pleaded Ava.

"We could ask him about his job too, couldn't we, Mama?" said Gracie.

"Let's see, shall we?" said Mother. "If he's not too busy, I'm sure he'd be happy to tell you his stories."

"Yay!" screamed the children. They were a noisy lot when they got excited.

As they wandered ashore they saw strange sheep. "These are Soay sheep," said Mother. "They are hardy and can cope with the harsh weather here. The soil in St Kilda, in the lower parts of the village, is very good and full of grass. This good soil has been helped by hundreds of years of spreading dung from the animals. In these old black houses, animals lived alongside humans all winter. In the spring they were put outside and a massive spring-clean involved scraping out all the animal dung from the house onto the fields," said Mother.

"Not very nice. In fact, that's pretty yucky," said Ava, scrunching up her nose.

Soay sheep.

Signs show who used to live here.

"Yes, I suppose so," said Mother. "But they lived successfully like that for thousands of years. This island was abandoned in 1930, but it is believed to have been inhabited as many as 4,000 years ago."

St Kilda was fascinating and the children learned all about the old ways of the people who lived there. Before long, they were back at sea. They saw all sorts of wildlife, and particularly loved the pod of dolphins, which was jumping all around the boat. The dolphins loved showing off!

Dolphins in the mist.

Skye helms the boat.

The weather had been misty since they had arrived at St Kilda, but suddenly the sun came out. Scotland was known for having four seasons in one day, and today was no exception. With the sun splitting the heavens, they went on their way to Mull, jumping on the dinghy that was stored on the foredeck and listening to Father tell the stories of the places they visited on the way, including the one about a man called Gavin Maxwell, who kept pet otters in a beautiful little bay called Sandaig. *Scotland is full of adventures*, thought Gracie, and she wished there was more time to explore!

Passing Ardnamurchan lighthouse – Tobermory is just round the corner!

Gordon the
Wildlife Filmmaker

It had been a mammoth voyage, full of wonderful things to see, learning about the wildlife and the olden days, and now the Mackenzie children had finally arrived at Tobermory. Gordon was waiting for them at the pontoon.

"Hello girls!" he called. "How was the sailing?"

"Great!" replied Gracie, who was always first to speak when new people were about. The twins looked on with interest while Mother chatted to Gordon.

"So, girls," he said. "I hear you've been seeing all sorts of wildlife on your adventures. Have you had fun?"

"Oh yes," said Ava shyly. "We've seen lots and lots of birds, plus dolphins jumping, seals and even the fin of a minke whale!"

"You have been busy!" said Gordon. "Your mother said that you have been investigating different jobs. Would you like to learn about my job?"

The children smiled in unison. "Yes, please!" they shouted.

"Do you have photos of tigers and things?" asked Ava.

"I think I can manage that," replied Gordon. "Let's go up to the house with your mum and dad, and we can have a look."

They all followed Gordon up the narrow, winding road through the painted houses of Tobermory. It was an idyllic little town, with each house painted a different colour. Skye wondered if they had to have a meeting to decide on who was painting their house what colour. There were lots of people on the shore, sitting on benches looking at the views. The harbour was buzzing with fishing boats and dinghies. It was just as Gracie had imagined.

The painted houses of Tobermory.

Gordon invited them in and the children had juice while the adults chatted. The girls were eager to find out what Gordon had been up to in his job. Mother had been teaching them about different jobs and the key things seemed to be to find something that you enjoy doing and to work hard. They wondered if Gordon's work was hard. *It must certainly be enjoyable,* thought Ava.

Gordon came over to them with his computer. On it, he had lots of pictures of exotic places and animals the girls had never seen.

A tropical moth.   A pit viper in Borneo.

The girls were fascinated. They flicked through the pictures with glee, jumping back excitedly at some of them, including Gordon with a bear!

Gordon with a black bear in the north woods of Minnesota.

"Yikes!" said Ava, "What *are* you doing?

"We became friends," said Gordon.

"There are eight types of bear in the world and this is a black bear. You can spot them from their black coat with a white patch on the chest. He is a friendly one! You mustn't approach bears if you don't know what you're doing, as they can be very dangerous," he warned.

Panda bears in Wolong, China.

"What kind of animals do you see when you are working?" asked Gracie.

"All sorts, including some that we didn't know existed! We are constantly finding new species of animals and insects. My work takes me all over the world from the tropical rainforest to the desert, and from the mountains of the Himalayas to the cold of the Arctic. The countries I visit depend on which animal I am looking for," said Gordon.

Gordon looking for wolves in northern Washington State, USA. Sled dogs are used to travel silently, rather than using snowmobiles, so that the wolves are not scared away. The only problem is that the dogs cannot carry people up hills, so Gordon had to run alongside the dogs for 17 miles. This was one of his most physically challenging jobs!

A mountain lion is *tranquillised* (given an injection to make it calm) before a health check.

"Have you got a favourite animal?" asked Ava.

"Lots of people ask me that and it's a really hard question to answer! It's a bit like asking whether you have a favourite person, because there are so many fantastic animals in the world that are unique and interesting in very different ways. I do have some favourites though. For domestic animals, I love horses for their beauty and for the interaction they have with people. I'm not so fond of zebras, however!

"I also love polar bears because all the animals that I film take me to varying degrees of discomfort, but the polar bear took me to the highest level. I respect them very much for their power and their ability to survive where humans cannot: in some of the harshest and most remote parts of the planet. I'm also a big fan of killer whales. Second to man, they are the most widespread mammal on the earth and there is still so much we don't understand about their way of life. They are impressive and intriguing creatures."

Taking the measurement of baby polar bears. Their ability to survive depends on their *emergence weight*, which is their weight when they come out of the den. Most are born around Christmas and emerge in late April.

Killer whales, northeast of Shetland.

"What is the most scared you have ever been?" asked Gracie.

Gordon laughed. "There have been lots of time that I have been scared. Sometimes, the journey to get to the places where the animals are located can be the most scary part of the trip! I was on a ship once, on my way to make a film.

"The ship was normally used for killing baby seals and was covered in all the grease and grime of a working boat. We were in the Arctic seas in the northernmost part of the world. It was freezing and we hit a two-day storm. The boat was heeled right over, pounding into the waves. The safest part of the boat was where they stored all the dead seals, so you couldn't go there to shelter. Luckily, I don't get seasick but it was terrifying. We had quite a strange Swedish captain and when he got scared, he just laughed. Sitting up was too uncomfortable and tiring, so in the end I just lay down. All I could hear from my bunk was the captain laughing his head off all night. At one point I got up and asked 'How far have we tipped over?' and he said, 'More than ever before!' He'd been sailing for over 60 years."

The girls didn't like the sound of the boat. They liked sailing, but they weren't so fond of really bad weather, especially Ava who got seasick.

"You worked with polar bears," said Gracie. **"Was that not scary?"**

Gordon laughed again. "Very much so, Gracie. Truly terrifying. I have been chased by many things, including tigers and bears, and have been really scared for short periods of time.

Gordon filming an Amur tiger in Russia.

An Amur tiger – the biggest cat on the planet.

"The polar bear, however, was forty minutes of prolonged panic. It is the most dangerous animal that I have ever worked with and the most scared I have ever been with animals! I was in a small plastic box in the Arctic, surrounded by ice.

"The idea was to be able to observe the polar bear in its natural environment. The trouble with polar bears, unlike most other animals, is that they see us as their next dinner! And they have a very strong sense of smell, thousands of times more powerful than ours.

19

Transporting the plastic box from the ship.

"This polar bear smelled me easily through the air gaps in the doors. I was expecting her to be curious, maybe to come and check me out, but instead she spent forty minutes trying to break into the box, with a view to eating me! The perspex was flexing and the box was rattling. I was very scared.

Transporting the box over the ice.

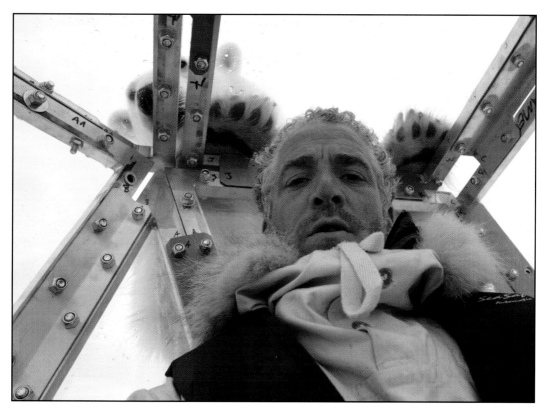

Gordon inside the plastic box.

Raaaaar! (Yikes.)

"It is our job to minimise risks and make sure we are all as safe as possible. However, the plastic in the box had never been tested to below minus forty degrees and I was worried it was going to shatter. I spent a bit of time asking myself, 'How stupid will this look if I die here?' In the end, after forty minutes of total terror, she finally gave up before she realised that there was no lock on the sliding door! The cameramen, who were 300 metres away using a long lens, were having a good laugh at me!

The polar bear wants to get inside!

"I had to speak really loudly for the camera as I could hardly hear myself think over the sound of my heart beating! It was the most dangerous thing I have ever done, but it was one of my lifelong ambitions. In the end, we got fantastic footage of Lyra, the mother polar bear, and her epic struggle to raise her two cubs, Miki and Luca, in the bitter conditions of the Arctic, where they were often close to starvation."

Ava, Skye and Gracie were speechless.

"Wow," said Skye. **"Did you not want to scream for help?"**

Gordon laughed again. "It was tempting!" he said. "However, this is my job. Yes, it was risky, but in my head I have a set of safety checks: 'what will I do if such and such happens?' There are a lot of people who get into trouble and lose their lives in the natural environment because something happens that they didn't see coming. It's up to me to stay safe and it's up to me to deliver the content for the programme, so unfortunately, screaming is not an option!

In the Arctic, happy to be out of the plastic box!

"At one point, when we were doing the polar bear series, one of the guys said 'It's not very funny. Can we jazz it up a bit?' I wasn't sure what to say. Much as I love a joke, we're not dealing with a hugely funny topic; it's baltic, uncomfortable and I'm not in top humour form! We had a good laugh, but the subject is serious when you see the struggle these animals have in the wild."

Transport to the Arctic can be tricky!

Filming from the edge of the glacier. Glacier ice is blue because it is so dense that it absorbs every other colour, so blue is the only colour we see!

The children were fascinated by Gordon's stories. *What an adventure!* thought Skye.

"Do you like animals or people better?" asked Gracie.

"It's a strange life that I lead, Gracie," said Gordon. "It's like two lives that don't cross over. Sometimes I'm not sure who is the real me – the one with the wife and two kids, or the one being bitten by insects and bears, hiding up trees. I am often more comfortable wandering in the woods of north Minnesota with black bears than I am cycling through the city on a Friday or Saturday night! I find animals more predictable, but I suppose that is because I am more used to dealing with them. I am very happy in both my lives and it's fantastic to come home and spend time with the family, but I also love the solitude of being out in the wild with nature. I'm lucky that I get to do both."

Living in the woods of north Minnesota with the black bears. This male bear is over ten years old. With bear hunting, life expectancy is around two years, so he has done well!

"How do you find the animals?" asked Ava.

"First, we research the animal to find out where we think they are likely to be. Sometimes, we are looking for animals in places where people don't believe they exist, which can make things a little more complicated. Some countries have very accessible wildlife. Scotland, for example, has some of the most accessible wildlife on the planet. Visitors to this country are often bowled over by how easy it is to see it.

"However, most of my trips overseas involve some kind of epic voyage to get to the natural habitat of the wildlife we want to film.

Unloading all the equipment. On sea ice, you can cover large distances on snowmobiles.

"We use all sorts of transport to get to different places, ranging from large ships and small canoes, to sea planes and helicopters, to ponies and walking. We always have a lot of heavy kit to carry, so it can be quite an exhausting trip.

Rafting on unexplored rivers for 'Expedition Alaska'. It took twelve days rather than the expected three, so they ran out of food and had to catch fish! None of the rapids had been mapped and sometimes they were so bad that they had to hike, carrying the two large rafts over the mountains.

Kayaking.

Being dropped off by seaplane in Alaska before descending the river.

Surveying the rim of a volcano in Papua New Guinea.

Helicopter landing in a small clearing in the jungle of Papua New Guinea.

Looking for high-altitude tigers in Bhutan, Himalayas. More than twenty ponies were used to carry heavy equipment through the mountains.

Sometimes travel by foot is the only way!

Filming barnacle geese in Svalbard - halfway between Norway and the North Pole.

Trekking in northern Washington State, near the Canadian border, looking for wolves.

"When we finally arrive at our destination, we look for signs of where an animal might have been. Paw prints in the mud or snow are an obvious thing to watch out for, but there are also more subtle signs that are easily overlooked.

"I found a wolf hair on a tree, which gave us a good idea that there were wolves in the area using the tree as a rubbing post. It is in places like these that we put a camera trap. Camera traps are little cameras, hidden as much as possible, which can film day and night. They are less intrusive than humans, as the animals can smell us and sometimes that scares them off. Camera traps can be put anywhere."

Looking for clues. Paw prints in the snow.

Big paw prints in the mud.

"What other places would you put a camera trap?" asked Ava.

"You just have to think like an animal and ask yourself 'If I were a tiger, where would I go?' Most big mammals tend to stick to a path or small trail, so if you are looking for leopards in a forest, you just have to look for these trails.

"Sometimes there are lots of open spaces. That doesn't work so well and you need to place a trap on top of a tree to see if you can find the routes that the animals take. When we filmed the tigers, we were in very steep-sided mountains so instead of putting the traps on a track, we put them on the ridges at the very top. Each situation is different and you have to assess your surroundings and look for clues. Camera traps are a very useful tool but to get great footage, we need to be doing it ourselves. That's why we often make hides and have to wait for a long time before the animal appears!" he smiled.

"What are the hides like?" asked Gracie.

"Each one is different as we need to try to blend in with our surroundings and avoid scaring the wildlife away. We often use a camouflaged tent but other times, we hide under branches or even at the top of trees.

Testing a hide.

Looking for wolves in British Columbia in the Great Bear Rainforest.

"When we film in the rainforest, the top of the trees is known as the *canopy* and the views are fantastic. It's a long way up and we have to hoist ourselves up on a rope and sit there for hours. This often results in being rained on and being bitten by various insects. There are so many insects in the rainforest. When I'm up there, I just hope that the bees don't come in their swarms. Flies I can cope with, but a bee swarm is not pleasant!"

A hide being hoisted up a tree in the rainforest of Papua New Guinea.

"What is the longest time you've had to wait in a hide?" asked Skye.

"The longest stretch was in a hide in Sierra Leone in West Africa. I was waiting for chimpanzees to appear at a nut-cracking site. I was in the hide all day, every day for two weeks. Camera traps were not around in those days so we had a lot more waiting to do!

"The worst hide I've been in was in Papua New Guinea. I was waiting for cassowaries, which are massive, emu-like birds. My hide was in a mosquito-infested swamp, hot and sweaty, with boggy ground and all sorts of biting insects. It was not pleasant! However, being in a hide is not always a bad experience. There are lots of times that I've slept out in Scotland, even in winter. Once you've had something to eat and you're warm, it's actually pretty comfortable.

"I'm not always living in the hide and I'm not always on my own. Depending on what we are filming, there can be a large group of us. We create a base camp and go out to explore from there. Conditions at base camp can actually be reasonably comfortable, although I suppose it depends on your idea of comfort!" laughed Gordon, showing them photos of him in a hammock in a cave.

Living in a cave covered in bat poo, miles from the nearest place to take a bath!

Sometimes lots of equipment is needed to make a film.

A long lens is used to film things that are farther away.

"How long are you away from home?" asked Ava.

"That totally depends on the job. The longest filming I've done was the black bears in northern Minnesota in America. The bear is a misunderstood animal. They tend to keep to themselves, but they are very inquisitive. A lot of big animals are scared of people so you can normally work out what they are going to do. However, the bears' curiosity makes them rather unpredictable. The phrase 'An elephant never forgets' is quite true as animals remember things that have happened to them. An elephant or a bear who has had a bad experience with humans will behave very differently to one who has not.

"I spent a year living in the woods with the bears, specifically following Lilly, a first-time mum with one little cub that we named Hope. Bears normally have several cubs but little Hope had no brothers or sisters. Lilly was a great mum, looking after Hope and playing with her. One day, she went off and didn't come back, leaving Hope all by herself.

Gordon with Lilly in Minnesota.

"We couldn't figure out why Lilly had abandoned her cub after putting so much effort into feeding and looking after her. Living in northern Minnesota is a hard life for bears. They only have six months to feed themselves before they go into hibernation for the winter. We think Lilly decided to go and get pregnant again so that she could return in spring with three cubs rather than just having one. It sounds quite harsh but we couldn't think of any other explanation.

Bear cubs.

"In the end, we decided to help Hope. Otherwise she would have starved. Lilly did get pregnant and was eventually reunited with Hope. The last time that I saw them, they were safe and sound in their den, ready for the winter. A happy ending!" he smiled.

"Do you enjoy your job?" asked Ava.

"I think I must be one of the luckiest men in the world," replied Gordon. "Yes, I love it. There are so many parts I enjoy that it is hard to summarise it. I love the solitude, being amongst nature and living beside the animals. I don't get complacent with what I see and I am equally in awe of the otters and dolphins that we see around Tobermory as I am with a brand new species that we might find in the rainforest. The animals in this world are truly amazing. I like being alone, but it is also really fun working as part of a team. For the big TV productions there are a huge amount of people working hard to make the programme as good as it can be.

Gordon enjoys the view from the top of a mountain in Minnesota.

"The challenge of surviving and achieving base levels of comfort with limited resources is also fun. I enjoy trying to find solutions to all the little challenges we face in each location. The simple experience of seeing new places, some very different to our home, is also something that you can never take for granted. The views, the people, the animals, the challenge of the job. I love it all," he continued.

Camping beside the retreating glaciers in Kenai Fjords, Alaska.

All new species found in the rainforest are recorded by the team.

"How do you become a wildlife filmmaker?" asked Gracie.

"Hmm," said Gordon. "Well, I didn't go the standard route. Instead I got very lucky and was in the right place at the right time. The formal route would be to study things like zoology, do a media course and perhaps biological imaging or something like that in order to become a wildlife cameraman.

The largest rat in the world!

"Lots of people have a passion for a certain type of animal and get work by being specialists in their field. Any work experience you can pick up when you are young always helps. It's important to be prepared to work hard and show commitment. That often means doing jobs you don't like, in order to get to where you want to be. It's really important to have a good attitude to work, which means doing the good jobs and the bad with a smile on your face!"

"How did you get into it, Gordon?" asked Ava.

"I always wanted to lead an interesting life and do something different. I grew up here on the Isle of Mull with my four brothers and sisters. Our mum looked after us, but she had two jobs so it was tough for her. I spent a lot of time outside and have always enjoyed wildlife and the great outdoors. I liked being with friends but I also liked being on my own. Mull is a perfect place for that – very similar to Badaneel in that respect. I didn't do well at school and spent most of my time daydreaming.

Thermal camera that picks up heat - used at night.

"Suddenly I got to fourth year and realised that I didn't have many options for my future. I got a job in a local restaurant and one of the owners was a guy called Nick Gordon, who was a wildlife cameraman. He used to come home from his travels with amazing tales of animals he had seen and places he had visited. I was fascinated by his stories.

"Luckily for me, he needed an assistant and I just happened to be about. My mum thought it was a great idea and so I headed off into the wild at the age of seventeen.

"We went to Sierra Leone in Africa and it was an awful year because I was desperately homesick all the time. One of my jobs was to build fifty-metre towers, which wasn't ideal as I had a bad fear of heights! I'd never been out of Scotland, but suddenly I was faced with dealing with the neighbouring chiefs and the politics in that area. It was eye-opening to say the least! The thing you learn about meeting people from very different cultures is that we might think they seem strange, but in fact we seem equally strange to them!

Locals in Papua New Guinea.

First bath after a week of trekking in the forest!

"I had to work hard but in the end, I got over being homesick and realised that Nick had given me the opportunity of a lifetime. He opened the door to the career I dreamed of. Soon, we were away on another trip to the Amazon region of Venezuela, looking for a tribe that was said to worship and eat the world's largest species of tarantula. These are massive, poisonous spiders. Not the kind we find in our bath at home! Nick and I managed to find them and so by the age of nineteen, I was sitting with a long-lost tribe, eating spiders! It was such an adventure, and still is.

Prayer flags flying in the wind in Bhutan, Himalayas.

"I spent five years as an apprentice with Nick and then started working on my own. There is so much unknown and a huge element of luck in my job, but with experience I have become good at reading the signs, and learning how animals behave. In the end, you build up a field-craft that is based on years of experience – including messing up!"

Fully loaded for the next adventure!

Filming in Patagonia, Chile, looking for pumas.

"Do you like doing the filming or the presenting better?" asked Ava.

"I like both. Someone once said to me that I would never be the person in front of the camera because I lacked passion and enthusiasm. I couldn't understand why they had said that, when I clearly did not lack either. It was just that I didn't show it as much as other people. Coming from Scotland, we have a culture of being modest and it is good manners not to blow your own trumpet, shall we say. However, I realised that if I was to be successful, I needed to show my enthusiasm. Initially I really didn't want to be in front of the camera. I hated it. But gradually, I found that there were as many opportunities in front of the camera as behind it. Now I really enjoy it and most of my time is spent presenting. I'd like to do a few more trips that involved being behind the camera, if only so I don't have to worry about having something hanging out of my nose!" he laughed.

The girls laughed too. *Gordon was very funny*, thought Gracie. *And what a cool job…although also quite scary!*

Life behind the lens.

"What is the worst part of your job?" asked Gracie.

"I miss fruit and vegetables, and a balanced diet. Recently in Burma, all we ate was rice and peanuts, which is not ideal when you are trekking all day!

Catching some sleep.

"The levels of physical hardship are quite high at times. I suppose I'm a bit like a kid; I always liked dares. I might not have been the best at Maths, English and so on but I loved a challenge. Out in the wild, each day is a challenge and my daily mission is to try to better my situation in any way I can. I get great satisfaction from small improvements in comfort levels!

Cooking with some locals in the Amur region of Russia.

"There are times when certain basic functions, like going to the toilet, are not possible! On one of my last trips, we were hiding in trees that weren't very tall. We were warned that if the elephants saw us, they might try to pull down the trees. We had to keep our pee in containers so as not to give away our position and were also advised to pee directly onto the elephant if it came near. Apparently that was supposed to dissuade it from coming after us!

"However, the very hardest part of the job for me is probably the same challenge that most people have: finding a work/life balance. I am away from family and friends a great deal. It is slightly different to most folk in that when I am gone, I am completely out of touch – no phone, no TV, no radio. I'm completely cut off, enjoying where I am but unable to easily communicate with home."

Camping in the snow of the Himalayas.

"How do you make money doing your job?" asked Skye.

"Most of the time, I sell my ideas to TV companies or TV contacts. Then I get paid for the days I work – known as the daily rate. All cameramen are paid on a daily rate and if you are good enough, you can work as many days as you want. Some are lucky enough to only work a few months each year, and have other businesses at home.

"My job is to convey the experience of seeing the animals in the wild and capture it through technology for delivery to the TV screen.

"The most important thing about work is that you enjoy it. You will find it easy to work hard if you're doing something you enjoy. Waking up to a new horizon is as exciting today as when I first started.

Filming humpback whales, penguins and fur seals in Patagonia, southern Chile.

Filming jaguars along a river in Guyana.

Bhutan, with the Himalayas in the background.

"Now then, I think it's time for a trip outside into this sunshine," said Gordon. "What do you think, girls?"

"Great idea," said Ava.

"Thanks for showing us all the pictures and telling us about your job!" shouted the Mackenzie girls as they ran into the garden, chattering about their latest encounter with the world of grown-up jobs. Finally they all reached the pontoon.

"Well girls," said Mother. "What do you think about being a wildlife filmmaker?" Mother could hardly hear herself think as the children all spoke at once, recounting Gordon's stories of elephants, polar bears and massive, deadly spiders. They were still at it as they got in to play in the dinghy. Mother heard them as they rowed around. "If you see a grizzly bear – play dead; a black bear – fight back; an elephant – drop something to distract it; a tiger – stand your ground and look as big as possible; a wolf – run towards it; a polar bear – you're stuffed!"

Ava, Skye and Gracie looking for sea creatures.

And so it went on with shrieks of laughter and excitement. Mother smiled. It was a big wide world out there, full of opportunity. She sat back with Father, Gordon and friends, enjoying the sunshine and the birds flying by, looking at the beautiful island of Mull.

The end.

What do the grown-ups do?

The books are available in paperback through all good bookstores as well as through www.troubador.com and other places online. For more information, please check the website **www.kidseducationalbooks.com**.

The What do the grown-ups do? series in order of publication:

Book 1: Joe the Fisherman

Book 2: Papa the Stockfarmer

Book 3: Sean the Actor

Book 4: Fiona the Doctor

Book 5: Richard the Vet

Book 6: Gordon the Wildlife Filmmaker

More coming soon!